8/22

"I loved this b... It inspired me to try
new things and enjoy more adventures."
Nina, age 9

"A wonderful, magical story. I liked the sna...
and the worm because they were funny."
Lucy, age 6

"I love how the Playdate Adventure Club saves
the planet one adventure at a time! It's cool
that the worker bees are girls. Girl power!"
Elsie, age 8

"As someone who doesn't love reading, I
found this book really fun, and I've learned
that pesticides are very bad for bees."
Seb, age 10

"A heart-warming, thrilling book with lines
_____ age."

Katy

Chatty, sociable and kind. She's the glue that holds the Playdate Adventure Club together. Likes animals (especially cats) and has big dreams of saving the world one day.

Cassie

Shy but brave when she needs to be. She relies on her friends to give her confidence. Loves dancing, especially street dance, but only in the privacy of her bedroom.

Zia

Loud, confident and intrepid. She's a born leader but can sometimes get carried away. Likes schoolwork and wants to be a scientist when she's older, just like her mum.

Luca

The newest member of the club. He's shy, like his cousin Cassie, but not when it comes to going on an adventure. Is obsessed with watching nature programmes.

Thunder

Big, white and fluffy with grey ears, paws and tail. He's blind in one eye, but that's what makes him extra special. Likes chasing mice, climbing trees and going on adventures. Is also a cat.

**Join the friends on
all their Playdate Adventures**

THE HONEYBEE TREASURE HUNT

Book Six

THE HONEYBEE

TREASURE HUNT

Emma Beswetherick

Illustrated by Anna Woodbine

ROCK THE BOAT

A Rock the Boat Book

First published by Rock the Boat,
an imprint of Oneworld Publications, 2022

Text copyright © Emma Beswetherick, 2022
Illustration copyright © The Woodbine Workshop, 2022

The moral right of Emma Beswetherick and the Woodbine Workshop
to be identified as the Author and Illustrator of this work respectively has
been asserted by them in accordance with the Copyright, Designs, and
Patents Act 1988

ISBN 978-0-86154-255-0 (paperback)
ISBN 978-0-86154-256-7 (ebook)

Printed and bound in Great Britain by Clays Ltd, Elcograf S.p.A.

This book is a work of fiction. Names, characters, businesses, organisations,
places and events are either the product of the author's imagination or are used
fictitiously. Any resemblance to actual persons, living or dead, events
or locales is entirely coincidental.

Oneworld Publications
10 Bloomsbury Street, London, WC1B 3SR, England

Stay up to date with the latest books,
special offers, and exclusive content from
Rock the Boat with our newsletter

Sign up on our website
oneworld-publications.com/rtb

For my sister, who may be allergic to bees,
but who's created a honeybee paradise
in her beautiful garden

CHAPTER ONE

"Can anyone tell me what a honeybee has six of?"

Ms Coco's class were almost at the end of a trip to the local Beekeepers' Association and their beekeeper guide was rounding the day off with a quiz.

Zia threw her hand in the air.

"Yes?" the beekeeper said.

"Legs!" Zia called out.

"Correct!" he replied with a smile. "Bees have six legs, like all insects. Now, this next question is harder. Can anyone tell me what a bee has *five* of?"

Zia's hand went straight up again, but she knew she wouldn't be asked a second time. She looked around the room – most of the class were staring silently at the floor.

"Luca," said Ms Coco, smiling encouragingly. "How about you?"

Luca looked momentarily terrified, until his cousin Cassandra gave him a nod and a thumbs up.

"Er...um...er...*e-eyes?*" he answered, but it sounded more like a question.

"That's right!" said the beekeeper. "Well done." But Zia was desperate to add a bit more detail. Her hand shot up in the air again. "Did you have a question?" he asked her.

"I just wanted to say that two of the eyes are in the middle of its face, like a human, but the other three are on the top of its head. That's why it can see so well."

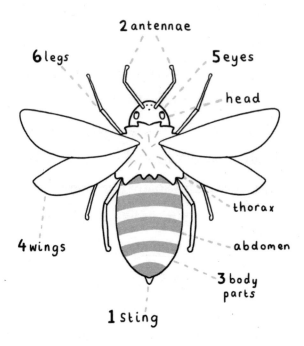

2 antennae

6 legs

5 eyes

head

thorax

4 wings

abdomen

3 body parts

1 sting

The beekeeper looked impressed, but Zia could feel the rest of her class fidgeting. She decided to let someone else answer the next question.

"What does a bee have *four* of?" asked the beekeeper, searching for someone else to throw up their hand. This time, it was Zia's friend Katy.

"Is it wings?" Katy asked. "Two small and two big?"

It didn't surprise Zia that Katy knew the answer. Katy *loved* animals more than anything (apart from her friends, of course) and knew a gazillion facts about them. Luca knew a lot too – he spent most of his spare time watching nature documentaries – but, unlike Katy, he was still nervous about speaking in front of his new class.

After three more questions – what do bees have three of (*body parts: head, thorax and abdomen*), two of (*antennae*) and one of (*a sting*)? – the beekeeper presented them each with a gift. Zia was delighted when she opened her paper bag to find a small pot of honey and an envelope containing wildflower seeds.

"Now you know how much work goes into producing even one spoonful of golden

treasure," said the beekeeper with a smile. By "treasure", Zia knew he meant honey. It's what he'd been calling it all afternoon. "And please sprinkle these seeds in your gardens, in pots or along a grass verge. Remember, without flowers, there would be no bees, and without pollinating insects like bees, we'd soon run out of food to eat!"

The children arrived back at school just in time to hear the final bell ring. Zia was bursting with excitement because her friends were coming back to hers for a playdate.

"That was fun," said Cassandra, fiddling with her curls. "I've been *terrified* of bees since I was stung last year, but it was cool learning about what they do."

"*So* cool," agreed Katy. "I won't be able to eat honey again without thinking about how it's made."

5

"Or look at f-flowers in the same way," Luca added, clasping his goodie bag tightly to his chest.

"Nor me," said Zia. "When we get back to my house, let's make some honey on toast. We can have a picnic in the garden!"

"Sounds yummy," said Katy, as Zia's dad appeared alongside the grown-ups gathering in the playground.

"Ms, can we go?" Zia asked their teacher. "Thanks for a fun trip!"

"Of course. Enjoy your playdate!" Ms Coco grinned.

"How was your day?" asked Zia's dad. "See lots of bees?"

But Zia and her friends were already rushing towards the school gates, desperate to get home and play.

It was a sunny afternoon in Zia's back garden, just a gentle breeze tickling the leaves on the trees. As her friends settled onto a large picnic blanket, Zia handed round plates of warm buttered toast, dripping with golden honey from their trip.

"*Mmmmmmmmm,*" said Zia, taking her first bite.

"This is *delicious,*" Cassandra agreed, licking the stickiness from her fingers. "My grandma makes this amazing Passover honey cake, but I've never tasted honey like this before."

"Me neither!" Katy exclaimed. "It tastes better than sweets."

"It totally does!" Zia grinned.

Luca nodded, then mumbled something with his mouth full to bursting.

"What was that?" laughed Cassandra. "I didn't hear a word you said."

"I said, 'I c-could eat this all d-day!'" Luca smiled, having finally swallowed his mouthful of toast. Luca had a stammer and sometimes found it hard to form words, which he said made him feel embarrassed. But he was more relaxed with his cousin and new friends than he was in class. He always seemed happy to join in their conversations.

"Hey, wouldn't you love to watch bees making honey for real," said Katy, spotting a bee buzzing past. "I mean, I know we were shown a hive today and told all about it, but how cool would it be if we could experience one up close and watch all the bees at work!"

"Katy, are you mad?" cried Cassandra, dodging the bee and darting to the other side of the picnic blanket. "Why would we want to get closer to stinging insects than we need to?

Didn't we see enough of them today?"

"I'm with Katy," said Zia. "Just imagine if we could shrink down so we're small enough to go *inside* a wild bees' nest. I don't think they'd sting us then." Zia paused for a second. "Hey, maybe that's what we could do on our adventure today. We could go on a hunt for some golden treasure!"

"I'm in," said Luca, putting a hand gently on his cousin's shoulder. "Remember what you told me on our last playdate, cuz, about the P-Playdate Adventure Club sticking together? There's s-safety in numbers, right? You'll be fine!"

"We might even get a new charm to add to our collection," added Katy, smiling reassuringly at her friend.

Cassandra thought for a second. She *did* love honey. And shrinking in size *did* sound fun. Maybe bees wouldn't sting them if they were insect-sized anyway? She'd also love a new charm to add to her bracelet. They'd collected five since they started the Playdate Adventure Club, although Luca only had one so far, which he kept on the wristband Katy had made for him. She wondered what the new one might look like.

"OK, I'll do it," she said finally. The others beamed. "On one condition. We only go if Thunder comes too."

CHAPTER TWO

Just then, there was a loud scrabbling sound. The four friends turned their heads to see a large white cat leap off the top of a fence post into Zia's garden.

"THUNDER!" they all shouted. "YOU'RE HERE!"

Thunder was Katy's ragdoll cat. He was as fluffy as a pillow, only had one eye and was "the most extra-special cat in the whole world", according to Katy. He was also the crucial fifth member of their Playdate Adventure Club.

"How d-does Thunder know how to f-find us, Katy?" asked Luca, as Thunder sauntered over and began brushing himself against their legs.

"I'm not sure," Katy answered. "But I'm glad he always does."

Everyone nodded, then reached out to ruffle Thunder's fur. On each of their playdates, it was like a sprinkle of magic rained down and turned their imaginary adventures into real-life amazing ones. Zia had been dreaming about what their adventure could possibly be today. Now she was even more excited for it to begin.

"Happy now, Cassie? The whole club is here!" She threw her arm round her friend's shoulder.

"Happy." Cassandra smiled, freckles dancing on her face.

"So, h-how are we going to go on this adventure? I mean, w-what do you think we need to do?" asked Luca.

On previous playdates, they'd either constructed something out of fabric or furniture or bits of recycling, or imagined something appearing that transported them to another world. They thought for a moment.

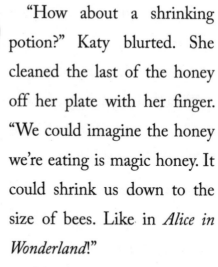

"How about a shrinking potion?" Katy blurted. She cleaned the last of the honey off her plate with her finger. "We could imagine the honey we're eating is magic honey. It could shrink us down to the size of bees. Like in *Alice in Wonderland*!"

"That could w-work," said Luca excitedly.

"And it's easier than jumping out of a window, like on our ocean adventure." Cassandra giggled.

"Much easier!" Zia was relieved Cassandra finally seemed to be enjoying herself. "OK, so first, why don't we eat a large spoonful of honey from our jars. Then we should close our eyes and imagine ourselves getting smaller and smaller while the garden gets bigger and BIGGER, until we're only a few centimetres tall! Are you ready?" she asked, picking up her spoon.

"Ready!" they shouted.

"Wait!" Katy cried. She stuck her finger into the honeypot and held it under her cat's nose. "Thunder, try this." He turned his head away. "Come on. Just a small lick." Thunder sniffed, then gently touched his tongue against the tip of her finger and pulled a face. "Yummy, hey?" she laughed. "OK, *now* we're ready!"

The four friends grinned at each other and nodded before swallowing large spoonfuls of honey. Then they grabbed hands in a circle around Thunder and closed their eyes tightly. Zia waited until all the honey had slipped down her throat – *mmmmm*, it really was *deeeeeeee*licious – before saying the magic words: "I wish to go on an adventure!"

"*I wish to go on an adventure!*" they all chanted.

To begin with, nothing happened. Was the shrinking potion even going to work? But after a few moments, a warm, syrupy feeling, rather like honey, started oozing from the tops of their heads to the tips of their toes. Suddenly, it was like popping candy was snapping and crackling through their bodies. Only when the funny sensations had stopped did they dare to open their eyes.

"OH!" cried Zia.

"MY!" squealed Katy.

"GOODNESS!" Cassandra screeched.

"THIS IS INSANE!" yelled Luca. "What's happened to the g-garden?!"

Except, the change *wasn't* to the garden. It just looked different because the four friends were now tiny in comparison to the world around them. The size of honeybees, in fact! The picnic blanket was a huge red and white chequerboard.

The plates looked like flying saucers and surrounding them was a forest of grass and twigs the size of climbing frames. They glanced up to see birds as big as aeroplanes swooping across a vast sky. The house was a giant's castle, the garden fence like the ramparts of a fortress.

Cassandra sighed. "This adventure's going to be trickier than we thought." She stared down at her teeny body. "Even crossing this picnic blanket is going to be hard."

"But b-brilliant," said Luca, checking to see that each of his body parts was still working.

"Katy, where's Thunder?" asked Zia.

They looked around, expecting to see a miniature one-eyed ragdoll cat licking his paw. But Thunder was nowhere to be seen.

"Maybe he's hiding," suggested Katy. "You know he gets a bit sulky when his transformations happen. Perhaps—"

But Katy stopped in her tracks as a dark shadow moved across them.

"What's that?" Cassandra cried.

They froze, stomachs churning. A fluffy grey-and-white monster was staring down at them with one piercing blue eye. The monster lifted its enormous paw, claws spread out, ready to swipe.

Everyone dived for cover under the nearest plate.

"Thunder!" Katy shouted from her hiding place. "It's me! I mean, it's us!"

"Katy, shush. He might hear us," whispered Cassandra, tugging at Katy's clothing to pull her back.

The white monster looked down at the plate and began to lower his fluffy grey head. He was licking his lips, looking very much like he was in the mood for a snack.

CHAPTER THREE

"He can't have eaten enough honey," Katy whispered, frowning. "That's why he's still big."

"*Please don't eat us!*" Cassandra screamed.

But just as Thunder brought his nose to the plate, searching to see where the four small scuttling creatures had got to, the smell of honey wafted into his nostrils. He dipped his paw into a jar and sat up again, lifting it to his nose for a sniff. His friends had disappeared after swallowing mouthfuls of this strange, sticky golden stuff. It smelled *horrible* and he didn't like the taste, but perhaps he should give it a go.

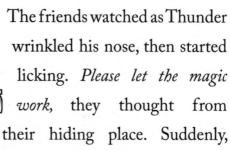

The friends watched as Thunder wrinkled his nose, then started licking. *Please let the magic work*, they thought from their hiding place. Suddenly, Thunder's whiskers went rigid, his tail shot in the air, his ears pricked up and his fur stuck out. Seconds later, the fluffy monster disappeared, to be replaced by a teeny replica cat, crouched on the rug in front of them, winking in confusion.

With a deep breath, Katy crawled out from under the plate.

"Thunder, we're over here!" she yelled, rising to her feet and waving her arms.

"I don't like being small," the cat said grumpily. "Small doesn't suit me." He sauntered over to Katy.

"I love that you're always so positive," joked Katy, scratching Thunder behind his ear.

"Sarcasm is the lowest form of wit, you know," Thunder retorted, as the others also appeared gingerly from under the plate.

"Were you really about to eat us?" asked Cassandra.

"Of course not," Thunder replied. "Although you'd probably taste nicer than that horrible gooey stuff. Ugh!" He pulled another face.

Katy laughed. "So what's the plan?" She turned to the others. "I don't think it's safe to stay here, out in the open."

"You're right." Zia thought for a moment. "Although I've no idea where we'll find a bees' nest."

"We could head further into the g-garden?" suggested Luca. "P-perhaps we'll find someone – or *something* – we can ask?"

They agreed this was the best idea and set off behind Zia. They were glad the sun had disappeared behind a large cloud. It was hot work climbing over the creases in the picnic blanket, and they had to take long detours around the plates and pots of honey. When at last they were standing at the edge of the rug, panting hard and staring out into a never-ending forest of grass, Zia reminded herself that playdate adventures were ALWAYS worth it in the end.

"Are you sure this is even your garden, Zia?" asked Cassandra. "It looks more like a rainforest." She clipped her curls away from her damp forehead.

"Forest adventures are the best, you know," said Thunder.

"Only because you love climbing trees," giggled Katy. "Perhaps you'd like to lead the way?"

"Gladly," he said, and bounded off into the undergrowth.

24

As they fought their way through the tall, thick grass, scrambling over log-sized twigs and navigating their way under or around fallen leaves, Zia felt like she was competing in one of those giant obstacle races on the TV.

"Hey!" Cassandra cried out. "Let me go!"

Zia turned to see her friend being attacked by a monstrous green plant.

"Don't panic, Cassie!" Luca yelled, running over. "It's just s-sticky weed. Here," he said to the others, "help me p-pull her off, will you?"

Luca held on to his cousin's feet and Zia and Katy took her arms, careful not to let their own clothes touch the plant. Then, gently, they pulled, until at last they were able to pry Cassandra from the sticky green trap.

"You should have followed me *around* the weed," Thunder said smugly.

"Thanks, Thunder," Cassandra muttered, picking a piece of sticky weed off her T-shirt dress. "I would have done if *you* hadn't been moving so quickly."

Thunder was about to rush off again when a line of black ants cut across their path. The ants were so focused on where they were marching, they didn't notice the five strange creatures hiding in the long grass.

"I wonder where they're going?" Zia whispered.

They were close enough to make out every detail of the robot-like insects, from their hard body armour to their fierce, pincer-like jaws.

Cassandra shivered. "They look like aliens from another planet."

"You know a-ants are important to the environment," whispered Luca. "As they march,

they b-break up the soil, making it easier for oxygen and water to reach the roots of p-plants. They also help to spread seeds and fight off predators. They're basically little warrior gardeners!"

"They're not so little now," Cassandra said, frozen to the spot in terror.

Like an army on patrol, the ants kept coming…and coming…and coming.

"Do you think they'll know where we can find a bees' nest?" asked Katy hopefully.

"Let's find out." Zia darted past Thunder and started waving her arms at them.

"Be careful!" Cassandra shouted.

The ants stopped marching and, all together, turned round, their eyes now on Zia.

"*Stranger*," they chanted.

Zia took a step forwards, trying to steady her shaking legs. "Yes," she said, putting up her hands. "I *am* a stranger. But I'm not here to harm you. These are my friends," she said, beckoning the others to join her.

"Hi," whispered Katy.

"Nice to m-meet you," Luca said nervously. "We w-wondered if you knew where we m-might find a bees' nest?"

"*Bees*," the ants chanted.

"We're looking for some golden treasure," added Zia.

"*Treasure*," the ants chanted, then turned and pointed towards the back of the garden.

"The treasure's that way?" But as Zia spoke, a deafening rumble boomed across the sky, followed by a blinding flash of light. The ants fell back in line and hurried away. A huge droplet of water splashed onto the soil only millimetres from where they had been standing.

"Over there!" shouted Luca, pointing to a large, circular blue thing resting at a slant on the ground.

They dived for shelter as the drops of rain turned into lashing torrents. The sky grew darker. The grassy soil around them became drenched with rainwater. Mud splashed against their clothes and Thunder's fur and they hoped with all their might that their honeybee adventure wasn't over before it had really begun.

CHAPTER FOUR

An enormous puddle of water was now forming at the entrance of their hideout and they all exchanged worried glances. They crept further backwards where the ground wasn't so flooded and waited for the storm to pass.

"What are we hiding under?" asked Cassandra, looking up at the blue shelter above their heads.

Luca reached up to touch it. "It feels like p-plastic," he said.

"It must be my sister's frisbee!" Zia exclaimed.

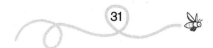

"Lucky for us it landed where it did."

When they didn't think it was possible for any more rain to fall from the sky, sunshine finally broke back through the clouds. The grey, soggy world turned green again, the droplets of water around them glittering and sparkling like diamonds.

"At last," Thunder sighed. "I hate the rain. It's too wet."

Katy grinned. "Then let's find somewhere dry." She ruffled Thunder's soggy head. "Any ideas how we get out of here?"

They peered out across the rain-soaked ground, which now looked more like a pond than a puddle.

"Could we swim across?" suggested Cassandra. She was the strongest swimmer in their year.

Katy shook her head. "I don't think Thunder

would like that. And it looks way too swampy."

"I w-wondered about using that," said Luca, pointing to a large green leaf curled up at the edges. Its stalk was wedged under the frisbee. "It would make a b-brilliant boat."

"Great idea, Luca!" Zia beamed.

They spaced themselves around the frisbee and lifted it a bit so Luca could free the leaf. Thunder, meanwhile, was pawing at a long, narrow twig on the ground.

"Thunder, you're a genius!" Katy called.

Thunder looked at her curiously.

"The twig. We could use it as a pole, like punting, when you push yourself along a river."

They tipped the rainwater out of the leaf, then carried it to the edge of the puddle and placed it gently on the water. Holding it steady, they climbed on board, the leaf wobbling one way, then the other. They had to be careful not to capsize it. But when it steadied itself, Luca used the twig to push them away from the side.

As they took it in turns to propel the leaf through the swampy marsh, the warm sun beat down, drying their damp clothes and making them sleepy. It felt good to relax after such a tiring trek across the lawn.

"I hope the ants were right about bees being this way," said Katy, stifling a yawn.

"Maybe they were tricking us," said Cassandra. "Like in the enchanted forest, when the animals tried sending us in the wrong direction."

"Why would the ants d-do that?" asked Luca.

"Perhaps they don't trust humans," Zia said. "You couldn't blame them, really."

"True. Remember what the beekeeper said about humans being to blame for the loss of honeybee habitats," Katy added. "It's why there aren't as many honeybees as there used to be."

Luca sighed. "C-come on, let's enjoy the adventure," he said, trying to cheer everyone up. "It's not every day you shrink down to the size of a b-bug!" He scooped up a buttercup floating past on the water. "Let's see who likes b-butter the most. I used to play this with Cassie all the time."

Luca brushed the water off, angling the yellow petals beneath his friends' chins one by one. But the flower head was so big their whole bodies turned a bright shade of yellow.

"We definitely like butter, then!" Zia giggled, plunging the twig into the water and driving their boat further forwards.

"Even you, Thunder!" Katy exclaimed.

Thunder glowered.

"Now it's your turn, Luca," Cassandra said.

She took the flower from Luca and held it under his chin. Just like the girls, his whole body also turned a bright shade of yellow.

"I love b–butter. But I love honey more," he said, laughing.

It was Katy's turn to steer them through the

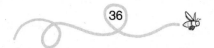

water now. She found it tricky at first, but soon settled into the rhythm of planting the pole down into the water and pushing off against the ground. But just as she was navigating around a patch of daisies, she spotted something scarily large up ahead.

"Woah – what's that?" she cried.

Everyone's eyes widened as they stared in the direction Katy was pointing.

"That must be Mum's rockery!" Zia blurted. "It's usually my favourite place in the garden. I love the different colours and shapes of all the rocks. It's like a miniature world. But now we're tiny, it looks impossible to climb."

"Maybe there's another w-way around," Luca said, holding on to the side of the leaf as he scanned the horizon. But the grass either side of their boat was turning muddy. There was nowhere else to go.

The rocks loomed over their tiny boat as Katy searched for the safest place to land. She heaved them onto what looked like a small gravelly beach, then, one by one, they climbed over the side of the leaf, scouring the rocks above for the best route to the top.

"Thunder, do you think you could climb up first?" asked Katy. "Careful, though – the rocks might be slippery from the rain."

Thunder didn't need to be asked twice. He leapt onto the lowest outcrop and began to climb.

"What's it like up there?" asked Cassandra.

"I can see rocks, but also paths around them," Thunder called down. "You'll need to climb up, but then it's easier. And I can see a stripy, buzzy thing flying between the flowers."

"A bee!" Zia grinned at the others, clapping her hands together excitedly. "Can't you hear it buzzing? Thunder, can you ask it if there's a bees' nest nearby?"

But Thunder didn't reply immediately, and then...

"Hey!" he yelled, sounding panicked. "You're getting a bit close. GO AWAY! I'M NOT A FLOWER! HEY, PUT ME DOWN! I'm..."

His voice got quieter and quieter along with the bee's buzzing, until they both disappeared into the distance.

CHAPTER FIVE

"Thunder!" everyone shouted.

Silence.

"THUNDER!" they yelled even louder.

"The bee must have taken him," said Katy in a panic.

"But how are we going to get him back?" Cassandra sniffed.

"They must have headed in that direction." Zia pointed towards the rockery.

"Didn't Thunder say there were paths on the other side of these rocks? If we climb up quickly, we might be lucky and catch sight of them."

While the four friends scrambled up the slippery rock face, Thunder was making a zig-zag flight through the air, stuck to the pollen sack on the bee's back legs. The buzzing was deafening. Thunder's whole body was vibrating with the sound. But something wasn't right – the bee seemed tired, incapable of flying in a straight line. Darting weakly to the left, then right, up, then down, then up again. The rollercoaster ride tied Thunder's stomach in knots. And the pollen, thick, sticky and coating Thunder's fur and whiskers, was now tickling his tiny nostrils.

A…A…

AAAAAAAAAA…

CHOOOOOOOOOOOOOOOOOOO!

For a cat so tiny, his sneeze was ENORMOUS. The bee jerked, then jerked again. Suddenly, Thunder was tumbling through the air before landing with a great THUD on a narrow path, just up ahead of Zia and her friends. They had finally finished their scramble to the top of the cliff.

"THUNDER!" they called out, rushing along the path towards him.

Thunder lay on the ground in a tangled mess of pollen and earth.

"He's not moving!" Katy gasped.

"If anything's happened to him…" cried Zia, her heart pounding.

Seconds passed that felt like hours. Was Thunder ever going to wake up?

Then: "This is *so* embarrassing," Thunder groaned, picking himself up and dusting himself down. "I hate being dirty."

"Oh, Thunder, I love you so much," cried Katy. She heaved him into her arms and covered him in kisses, which he swatted away with his paw.

"I'm so glad you're OK," Cassandra said, rubbing Thunder along his grubby back. "That was quite a scare you gave us."

"And quite some ride you had!" Zia breathed out deeply.

"That bee was flying very strangely," said Thunder.

"Yes, we s-saw you from the top of the cliff,"

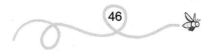

said Luca. "She seemed sort of…d-dizzy. Like she couldn't fly straight. Do you think we should s-see if she's OK?"

"I think we should definitely try and find her," Katy replied.

"But we don't have a clue where she went," Cassandra added.

The rockery was like a mountain range of towering peaks and narrow valleys. There was a maze of paths winding around the base of each mountain, dotted with flowers and spiky cacti.

"Do you think we'll *ever* reach the end of our treasure hunt?" Cassandra sighed  as she edged her way around a cactus, careful not to get speared by the spikes.

Zia took her friend's hand in her own. "First we find the bee and check on her. Then we look for her nest. OK?"

"Right," Cassandra replied, squeezing Zia's hand in return.

They'd been walking for ages and had just avoided being spiked by another cactus, when a pink head poked out from the earth in front of them.

"Hello!" it said.

"Hello!" Another head appeared round the corner of a rock. This one was brown, with wiggling antennae, and as it slid further into view, they saw it had a spiral shell on its back.

"A snail!" cried Luca cheerfully. "And an earthworm. H-hello!"

The two creatures stared curiously at them.

"What have we here?" said the worm. It spoke slowly, like it was running out of battery.

48

"The strangest minibeasts I ever saw," said the snail, competing with the worm to see who could talk the slowest.

Luca took a step forwards. "Hi, I'm Luca. And this is Zia, Cassie, Katy and Thunder. We're h-humans."

Thunder coughed.

"Sorry, humans *and* a cat."

"We've eaten some magic honey and now we're the size of bugs. See!" Katy spun round to

show herself more clearly. "We're on a treasure hunt and—"

"Woah! Slow down," said the worm.

"What's the hurry?" said the snail. "Tell us about yourselves."

Zia felt impatient to get going. "We'd really love to stay and chat," she said, "but there's a honeybee that needs our help."

"A honeybee?" asked the worm.

"Interesting," said the snail.

"What's wrong with it?" asked the worm.

Luca took a deep breath. "It seemed sort of d-dizzy," he said.

"Well, I haven't seen a bee today," said the snail.

"Nor me," said the worm, rotating his pink head. "Not since the lavender bush on Tuesday. Or was it Wednesday? I can't remember."

"All this fuss over bees," said the snail. "What

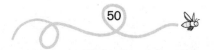

makes them so special?"

"Lots of things," Zia replied. "But I'm afraid we don't have time to explain now. Are you sure you haven't seen a bee?"

"What about us?" asked the worm, ignoring what Zia was saying.

"We're also important," agreed the snail.

"We decompose things," said the worm.

"And improve the soil," added the snail.

"If my tail gets cut off, I can grow it back," said the worm.

"Snails have more teeth than any other animal," said the snail.

"We really are fascinating creatures," said the worm.

"Yes, well, that's brilliant, and we'd love to hear more," said Zia. She was impressed by these facts, but her friends were now glaring at her as if to say, *Let's go!* "But I think it's time we found that bee."

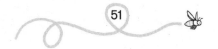

"It really was *lovely* to meet you," said Katy, as the gang of five edged past the worm and around the snail.

"Wait!" said the snail. They all froze. "Unless the creature on the other side of that rock is a bee?" He wiggled his antennae towards the mountain behind him.

"Oh yes," said the worm. "I remember seeing it now. A sorry-looking thing."

The adventurers' eyes lit up and they beamed in gratitude before charging off along the gravel path. "Too much of a hurry..." they heard the worm and snail muttering to each other as they turned the corner – where they spotted something curled up on the ground ahead. They approached cautiously, careful not to scare it. And that's when they noticed its black-and-yellow stripes and the wisps of white and grey cat fur sticking to its back legs.

CHAPTER SIX

"Hey there," Zia whispered.

It felt amazing to see a honeybee this close. Her colours were bright and vivid, but her eyes were heavy, her wings fragile and waterlogged.

"Can you hear us?" asked Katy gently.

The bee tried to raise her head, then lay back down, faint and exhausted. "I recognise you," she whispered, glancing at Thunder hiding behind Katy's legs. "I didn't mean for you to get stuck to my pollen sac. I hope you're not hurt."

Thunder smiled and shook his head, then came and rested his paw softly between her eyes.

"C-can you tell us what's making you dizzy?" Luca asked.

The bee's eyes darted between them as she took in the group gathered round her. Then, taking a deep breath, she started to speak. "I'd been collecting pollen and nectar." She coughed a few times with the effort of talking.

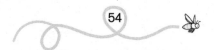

"Somewhere new. A field, not far from here. So many flowers. I stayed a long time. My head felt fuzzy. I couldn't fly straight. Everything went blurry..."

"But it doesn't make sense," said Katy, stroking the bee's furry abdomen.

"What d-do you think made you c-confused?" asked Luca.

The bee wheezed in and out, trying to calm her breath. "That's what I've been trying to figure out," she coughed. "I collect pollen and nectar every day. It's what worker bees do."

"You visited a field," said Zia. "One that you hadn't visited before?" She turned to her friends. "Maybe that's what's different about today. Remember the beekeeper talking about pesticides and how they can be harmful to bees? What if the crops in that field have pesticides on them? What if, by collecting pollen and nectar, the honeybee swallowed some? Could that be what's making her sick?"

"Pesticides?" asked the bee. Her eyes were closing now.

"They're what farmers put on their crops to stop insects eating them," Katy explained.

"Some g-gardeners use them too," Luca added.

"A lot are harmless," said Zia, crouching to stroke the bee's head. "But some have ingredients that make you sick. We must get you home to rest."

The bee coughed long and hard. "That's the problem. I can't remember where home is."

Think, think! They all scratched their heads, desperate to come up with a plan.

Then: "The worm mentioned a lavender bush, didn't he?" Cassandra glanced at Zia, eyes wide and hopeful. "Is there a lavender bush in your garden?"

"Yes, at the back, near the shed," Zia answered.

"So, if we head to the lavender bush, maybe we'll meet –" Cassandra turned to the bee, "– sorry, we haven't asked your name."

"Adira," the bee coughed. "It means strong. Although I'm not so strong now."

"Maybe we'll meet Adira's family," Cassandra continued.

"And maybe *they'll* know the way to the nest!" Zia exclaimed, finally catching on to the plan.

"Exactly!" Cassandra beamed.

"Excellent plan, cuz," said Luca. "Even if the b-bees aren't related to Adira, they m-might know where she lives."

"But how are we going to carry her?" asked Katy.

"Could we take it in turns?" asked Zia. They were near the end of the rockery now, although

Zia knew it was still a long way to the lavender bush. Carrying Adira wouldn't be easy.

Katy was about to respond when there was movement behind them. The snail and the worm were sliding slowly along the path.

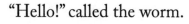

"Hello!" called the worm.

"Hello!" called the snail.

"You've found the bee," said the worm, wriggling up to join them.

Here we go again, thought Zia. But suddenly she had an idea.

"Snail, do you think you could carry this bee on your back? We need to take her to the end of the garden."

"As quickly as p-possible," Luca added.

"Quickly?" said the snail. "Snails don't do quickly."

The worm nodded and winked at the others. "Snails are sleepy creatures. They can sleep for

three years, you know. But you could come through the earth with me?"

Everyone shivered at the thought of a dark journey through the earth. Maybe this wasn't such a good idea after all.

"It's fine." Zia shrugged. "We'll figure something out. But thanks anyway."

Everyone went quiet, their eyes turning to the floor as they tried to think of a new plan.

"Unless…" said the snail, staring at the sorry group in front of him. He turned to the worm. "There might be something in our collection that could help?"

"Collection?" asked Katy curiously.

"Oh, it's nothing really," said the worm.

"Just some lost-in-the-garden things," said the snail.

"We'll show you," said the worm, "if you like?"

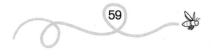

The worm and the snail slid past Adira and stopped by a gap in the rock. The others followed, hoping the collection wouldn't turn out to be a waste of time. But they were surprised to find a messy jumble of bits and bobs packed tightly inside a cave.

A button, a tennis ball, a clothes peg, a piece of string, the end of a skipping rope.

Zia's eye's darted around, amazed by what she was seeing. And that's when she noticed something large and colourful poking out from the assortment of lost objects. It was metallic red and blue, with orange flames down the side.

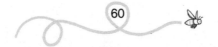

"My toy car!" she shrieked. "I lost this years ago. Look," she said to the others, pointing to a metal key sticking out from the back. "It's a wind-up one. It goes *really* fast."

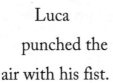

Luca punched the air with his fist.

"This is b-brilliant, Zia. We can all r-ride on this, including Adira."

"Oh yes, I'd forgotten about the car," said the worm slowly.

"Would you like it?" said the snail with a smile. "You seem like a trustworthy bunch."

"Yes, please!" everyone cried, clapping their hands in excitement.

As the worm and snail began manoeuvring the car out of the cave, the others ran back to where Adira was still curled on the ground. She looked worryingly weak now – there really wasn't much time. Standing two either side, Luca linked hands with Cassandra at Adira's head, while Katy linked hands with Zia near her sting. They bent down low and slid their arms under her thorax and abdomen, careful not to get stung. Then, as gently and as quickly as possible, they carried her towards the cave.

CHAPTER SEVEN

The toy car was waiting for them on the gravel path and they placed Adira hastily inside. The windscreen was cracked and there were large dents along the bumper, but the worm and snail proudly declared they were sure it worked "just fine".

"Cassie, why don't you drive?" suggested Zia.

"Me?" Cassandra said, fiddling nervously with her curls. "But you *always* drive."

"That's why it's someone else's turn." Zia smiled.

"I know you c-can do it, Cassie," Luca encouraged her.

"You've been brilliant today," Katy agreed.

So while Cassandra climbed anxiously into the driver's seat, in the back, the others took it in turns to lean over and wind the key on the back of the car. Thunder was tucked into the front passenger seat, keeping Adira company. The snail and worm were watching curiously from the path.

"CASSIE, READY?" shouted her friends from the back.

"Ready!" Cassandra cried, gripping the steering wheel tight and focusing on the path ahead. "Thunder, try and keep Adira safe, OK?"

Thunder nodded, putting a protective paw over the bee's abdomen.

"Don't drive too quickly," warned the worm.

"Slow and safe is best," the snail agreed.

"Right," said Luca. "I'm g-going to release the key in THREE...T-TWO...ONE...!"

Luca let go and the car shot forwards. It accelerated so fast, Cassandra struggled to keep them in a straight line. They bumped over the earth, zooming ahead towards the back of the garden. The world went past in a blur. They left the rockery in seconds and now long fronds of grass brushed past them as the car hurtled across the lawn towards the lavender bush. Cassandra kept her eyes focused on the ground ahead, knuckles white on the steering wheel.

They were almost at the end of the garden when the wind-up mechanism began to run down. The car slowed and the world came back into focus. They could smell the lavender and hear the hum of bees even before they spotted them buzzing around the purple flowers.

"We made it!" Zia shrieked, hopping over the side of the car and running to the bush.

"Brilliant driving, Cassie!" Katy called, as they all charged as fast as they could to catch up with their friend.

"Help, over here!" they yelled, fighting to be heard above the buzzing. "HERE! WE'RE DOWN HERE!" they shouted louder, waving their arms and trying desperately to be seen.

Only one bee, low down on the lavender bush, noticed the friends waving and calling. She flew down from her flower to land on the ground beside them.

Zia stepped forwards. "Please, your friend is hurt," she said in a frightened voice.

"She's over there, in the car," added Cassandra.

"We think she's been p-poisoned," Luca explained.

Katy beckoned for the bee to follow.

They hurried to the car, where, curled up next to Thunder, Adira was looking weaker than ever. Thunder was stroking her head with his paw, a worried frown on his face.

The worker bee gasped. "That's Adira," she cried. "Our sister!"

"I'm afraid she won't make it if we don't get her home to rest soon," said Cassandra.

The bee nodded and flew off again back towards the lavender bush. Within seconds, a swarm of bees was forming a circle around the car.

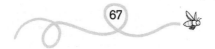

"We need a large leaf," said the leader of the swarm, who introduced herself as Melina.

Everyone searched around until Katy spotted just the one. "There, by the lavender!" She ran over to a long, wide leaf that was poking out from under the bush. Grabbing it by its stalk, she dragged it over to the car.

"That's perfect," said Melina. "Come, let's lay Adira on top."

Once more, they gently lifted the dizzy honeybee from the car and set her carefully on top of the leaf. Immediately, six bees spaced themselves round it, holding on to the edges of the leaf with their mouths before hastily taking off into the sky.

Katy turned to Melina. "Is your nest far away?" she asked.

"Not far. It's behind that wooden blue thing."

"You mean the shed?" Zia asked.

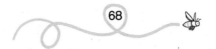

"Is that what it's called?" said Melina. "There's a tree behind it, in the corner of the garden. Our nest is in there."

"I had no idea!" Zia exclaimed. "There's really a nest in my garden?"

"Would you like to see?" asked Melina. "You could say hello to our queen. We'd love her to meet the minibeasts who saved Adira. Her name's Caspara. She's really kind."

Zia looked at her friends, who were smiling and nodding enthusiastically.

"We'd love to. Thank you." Zia grinned. But then a concerned look crossed her face. "Except none of us can fly."

"Then hop on!" said Melina, signalling for other bees to join them.

"On your backs?" asked Katy, worried they'd be too heavy for the bees.

"Where else?" Melina smiled, as one by

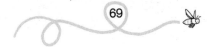

one, Zia, Katy, Cassandra, Luca and Thunder climbed on and wrapped their arms (and paws) round the bees' necks.

"Hold on tight." The bees began to beat their wings until they were lifting off the ground and flying up, up, up into the sky.

"WEEEEEEEEEEEEEEEEEE!" cried Zia as her bee zoomed even higher.

"THIS IS AMAZING!" shrieked Cassandra, as hers did a loop-the-loop.

Thunder's bee was carrying the lightest load. It was showing off, weaving in and out of all the others. "I'm an expert at flying, you know," Thunder called.

Everyone laughed.

"An adventure just *wouldn't* be the same without you, Thunder," Katy called back.

"I know," Thunder replied, making them laugh again.

They were flying through a narrow gap behind the shed now. The tree was just up ahead. As they flew closer, they could make out a line of bees gathered round a small opening in the trunk.

"They're the guards," said Melina. "It's their job to keep intruders from entering the nest. But you're with us, so you'll be OK. Just remember to duck!"

One by one, the bees whizzed through the small opening in the bark. The guards saluted as

71

they flew past, then they all came to land inside a warm, dark hollow. The friends dismounted and eagerly followed the bees, crawling through another small gap in the wood.

What greeted them on the other side was like nothing they'd ever seen. A magical glow so dazzling that they had to shield their eyes from the blinding light.

It was bright and shining and golden.

They'd found it at last. They'd found the golden treasure.

CHAPTER EIGHT

On their school trip earlier that day, they'd been shown the inside of a man-made beehive, but that was nothing compared to experiencing a bees' nest in the wild.

Deep inside the trunk, hidden from the outside world, huge vertical columns of perfectly formed hexagons towered above them like a magical palace made of gold. Some were dripping with sweet golden honey. Others were used as tiny hexagonal bunkbeds for baby bees to grow from their larva.

"Can we see Adira?" asked Zia eagerly, turning to Melina.

"You can, but there's someone we'd like to introduce you to first."

Hundreds of bees were crowding round now, curious to meet the five strange minibeasts who had rescued their sister and been invited into their home. They were pushing to get to the front, hoping for a quick glance, until suddenly they stopped, parting in the middle like a black-and-yellow stage curtain to make way for—

"The queen!" Katy squealed.

They bowed their heads as the queen came over. She was bigger and grander than the other bees in the nest, glowing a majestic golden yellow.

"Greetings!" she said. "I'm Caspara – it means 'protector of the treasure'. After all you've done for Adira, it's wonderful to meet you."

"Your majesty," said Zia, stepping forwards with a small bow.

"Thank you for having us." Katy beamed.

"Your nest is magical," said Cassandra.

"Like a c-cave of wonders!" Luca exclaimed.

Caspara nodded appreciatively. "You know, it's taken us three months to build it."

"We learned about hives today at school," said Luca excitedly. "Is it true that in every h-hive there are t-two types of bees, as w-well as the queen?"

"You mean workers and drones?" said Caspara. "Yes. Workers are female and do all the hard work. They build and guard the hive, pollinate flowers and collect nectar to turn into honey. The drones are male and keep my bloodline going. But every bee – there are thousands of us, you know – has an important job to do. That's why rescuing Adira means so much to us."

"Caspara," said Luca. "How is Adira? Is she g-going to be OK?"

The queen smiled. "She'll be fine. Thanks to all of you. Would you like to see her now?"

She ushered them into another towering chamber of golden honeycomb where, nestled cosily in one of the lower hexagonal bunks, was Adira, fast asleep.

"She looks so peaceful," said Katy. "I'm so relieved we got her home in time."

The queen looked serious for a moment. "Most humans don't understand how important bees are. But Adira is safe now. We've given her water and honey and she'll sleep until she's strong enough to work again."

"I'd always thought bees made honey only so *we* could eat it," Cassandra muttered, a blush creeping across her freckles.

"No, honey is *our* treasure," answered Caspara. "It's what gives us life. But, of course, we're always happy to share."

"Your majesty?" said Zia, a hopeful expression on her face. "Do you think we could help you make some honey? It's one of the reasons we came on this adventure. We'd love to learn more about how it's made."

Caspara glowed an even brighter gold. "It would be a pleasure," she said, then turned and crawled back out of the chamber, the friends following close behind. The first honeycomb chamber was now a hive of activity. Thousands of bees were busily moving round the small waxy hexagons. Not one of them was standing still.

"What are they doing?" Zia asked.

Caspara broke into a wide smile. "Some of the bees are doing a waggle dance. See how they're moving in a circle and wiggling their stings? Their movements help tell us where good supplies of pollen and nectar can be found."

"That's incredible," said Katy.

"It is, isn't it?" agreed Caspara. "But that's not all. The others you see are making honey. The nectar that worker bees collect from flowers is turned into a sugary liquid in their stomachs. When they arrive at the hive, they pass this liquid to other worker bees to swallow, where the process happens again. Finally, the liquid is deposited into the honeycomb, where workers beat their wings to evaporate the water. Honey is the treasure that's left over."

"Amazing!" Cassandra exclaimed. "Seeing it happen up close really is something else."

"Come on," said Caspara, smiling. "We'd never say no to five more workers in the hive."

They followed Caspara over to where a swarm of bees was gathered round a glistening tower of honeycomb.

"If you stand by your own cell, when a worker drops her digested nectar into the hole, I'd like you to fan your hands as quickly as you can. Like this," she said, turning her back and frantically beating her wings. "It's like our very own heating system. Why don't you give it a go?"

They practised fanning their hands quickly, although Thunder wasn't *quite* so fast at waving his paws.

"That's it!" Caspara enthused. "You've got it. Now spread out and watch the magic happen."

The five friends chose a hexagon each and waited while the worker bees dropped liquid into the cells. Then they started flapping their hands (and paws) to warm the air around it.

The change didn't happen straight away. It seemed to take forever, as more and more bees deposited liquid into the honeycomb. Their arms were getting tired now, until very slowly – and as if by magic – they saw the pale, runny liquid gradually transforming into thick, golden honey.

"You did it!" Caspara exclaimed excitedly. "Now, quickly, let's close the cells to keep the honey inside. The cells are our treasure chests, you see – treasure chests filled with delicious liquid gold. Watch – it's another of our magic tricks."

The queen stood aside as a swarm of worker bees crowded around the honeycomb. Small flakes of wax were visible on some of their abdomens, while the others nibbled at the flakes and began chewing them in their mouths.

"The younger bees have a special wax-producing gland," Caspara explained. "It converts sugar from the honey into the waxy substance you see on their bodies. The other bees chew the wax until it's the right texture, then use it to build honeycomb and cap each of the honey cells once they're full. Why don't you have a go?"

Caspara showed them how to remove the waxy flakes from the bees' abdomens, careful not to harm them. Then, cautiously, they popped the pieces of wax into their mouths and began to chew. Even Thunder decided to give it a try.

"I'm not sure about this," he mumbled, pulling another face.

"Keep chewing," encouraged Caspara. "It doesn't take long."

They chewed until they couldn't chew any more, then spat the softened wax back into their hands.

"Now watch," said Caspara, as a group of worker bees showed them how to mould the wax into a lid and secure it tightly over their honey cells.

"I never knew bees could do this!" Cassandra smiled, pushing her piece of wax into place.

"Bees can do many things," said Caspara proudly. "Is there anything else you'd like to know?"

Thunder was curled on the floor now, his one eye closed, exhausted by the day's ordeal. But everyone else was captivated by the continued hive of activity around them. They realised there was so much more left to learn.

CHAPTER NINE

"I have a question," said Cassandra, gazing admiringly up at the queen. "We learned about pollination today. But I'm not sure I understand the difference between nectar and pollen."

"Yes, I see why that's confusing." Caspara nodded. "I'll try and explain. Flowers are important to bees because of nectar *and* pollen. We change nectar into honey, as you've just seen. But we also eat pollen for protein and other nutrients. Pollination is the *side effect* of our flower foraging. As a bee lands on a flower, the pollen sticks to the pollen sacs on her back legs. When she moves on to the next flower, the pollen from the first flower transfers to the second flower. It's how flowers reproduce. Clever, don't you think?"

Katy nodded her head. "So *that's* how Thunder got stuck to Adira's back legs!"

"Exactly." Caspara grinned. "Each worker bee can carry their own body weight in nectar and pollen. We're a lot stronger than we look!"

"I have another question," said Zia, excited to be learning such interesting facts from the queen bee herself. "We were told today we'd run out of food without you, but I'm not sure I understand why."

Caspara looked at them with a serious expression on her face. "Another good question," she said. "And it's linked to the first. If bees – or other pollinating insects – didn't pollinate flowers, many plants that rely on pollination wouldn't reproduce and would gradually die out. Humans eat plants – think of many of your delicious fruits and vegetables, such as strawberries and cucumbers – and so do some of the animals humans like to eat. Did you know that about a third of the food you eat is thanks to bees? So if there weren't any bees, a lot of the foods you eat would no longer be available. We're the world's most important pollinator of food crops."

"Which is why you need p-protecting!" Luca burst out. "The plants need *you* to survive and we need *plants* to survive!"

"Yes!" Caspara beamed. "You've already seen what can happen when pesticides are swallowed by bees. But this isn't the only danger. Meadows are sometimes cleared to build new roads, and fields are turned into housing estates.

Every flower destroyed is one less flower for us to pollinate."

"*Now* I understand!" Katy exclaimed.

"And me," said Cassandra. "From now on, I'm going to cherish every flower that I see."

"Hey, I have an idea," said Zia. "Why don't we plant our wildflower seeds when we get home?" She turned to Caspara. "The more flowers in our gardens, the more nectar you'll be able to collect, right?"

Caspara nodded. "Right," she said. "That really would be wonderful. But now, I'm afraid we're going to have to say goodbye. Bees *always* have work to do. Where do you think the phrase 'busy bee' comes from!"

"That's so cool." Katy smiled. "But I really hate this bit." She looked gloomily around at everyone. "It's horrible saying goodbye to new friends."

"And we're going to miss you too," said Caspara sadly. "You've saved Adira. You'll *always* be welcome in our hive. Here, I have something for you." She signalled to two nearby worker bees who scurried off, then appeared seconds later with five small honeycomb pieces in their mouths. "Please, take these pieces of treasure with you, so you'll always remember us – and the magical connection between flowers, bees and animals."

"Thank you!" said Katy.

"I p-promise I won't forget," said Luca.

"Nor me," cried Cassandra.

"Nor me," echoed Zia, safely pocketing her piece of golden treasure.

Everyone said their goodbyes, then Zia held out her hands, pulling her best friends into a circle. Thunder was still fast asleep, curled on the ground between them. "Now, everyone, close your eyes and imagine you're back in my garden." She thought fondly about the picnic they were having. Her dad and sisters in the house. Her mum busy at work. "Then repeat after me: I wish to go home."

"*I wish to go home*," they all sang out.

Immediately, their bodies started fizzing and popping. They went boiling hot, then freezing cold, then tingly all over – like all the particles in their body were growing and stretching back to a regular size. Only when they'd returned to normal did they slowly open their eyes.

They were back on the picnic blanket, crusts of soggy toast scattered beside them. Thunder had woken and already scampered off, meowing and chasing a butterfly across the lawn. At the back of the garden was the lavender bush, buzzing with activity. Zia stared at her friends, blinking as she tried to get used to the size of the world around them. That's when she felt the tiny piece of honeycomb in her pocket and brought it out, slowly opening her hand.

"It's solid gold!" she gasped.

"It must be another charm!" Katy cried.

Katy was holding two, one for her and one for Thunder to keep on his collar. She leapt from the rug and began chasing him round the garden.

"Thunder, come here!" She giggled.

Soon, all four friends were up and running, laughing and jangling their charms in the air as they chased Thunder round the lawn. Eventually, he collapsed in a tired heap by the lavender bush, winking up at the buzzing bees with his one blue eye. Katy ran over, followed by the others, and clipped his charm to his collar. Then they all stood staring at the bees buzzing round the purple flowers, busily getting on with their work.

"I'm not scared of bees anymore," said Cassandra. "They might even be my favourite insects."

"They're d-definitely mine," Luca agreed, putting his arm round his cousin's shoulders.

"Who wants to plant some wildflower seeds?" asked Zia, and everyone nodded. "They'd look pretty all around the shed. Come on!"

They were just emptying their packets of

seeds when a honeybee buzzed past. It danced around their heads for a while before taking its tour of the garden. Had they looked more closely, they might have seen it hover for a second above a line of ants crossing the path, then whizz towards the lavender bush, past a snail and a worm trailing through the grass. They might even have spotted a few wisps of cat fur stuck to the back of the bee's legs.

But right at that moment, they were too busy dreaming about golden treasure to notice.

★ THE PLAYDATE ★
ADVENTURES

How to Plan Your Own
Playdate Adventure

1. Decide where you would like to go on your adventure.
2. Plan how you would get there. Do you need to build anything or imagine yourself in a new land?
3. Imagine what exciting or challenging things might happen on your adventure.
4. Decide if you are going to learn anything from your adventure.
5. Most important of all, remember to have fun!

BEES

Did you know…?

There are three types of bee in every nest or hive. Workers are female and the busiest, building the hive, collecting pollen and nectar and making honey. Drones are male and their role is to mate with the queen. The queen is the biggest bee in the hive. She can live for up to six years, laying eggs and producing special chemicals that tell the other bees how to behave.

If a queen bee dies, the workers create a new queen by selecting a young lava and feeding it a special food called royal jelly. The young bee will develop into a fertile queen.

Honeybees are exceptional fliers. They fly at around 25 kilometres per hour and beat their wings 200 times per second.

Young worker bees convert the sugar in honey into wax, which oozes through their abdomens. Beeswax has been used throughout history for making candles, waterproofing materials, polishing wood and leather and even in make-up!

Bees play a crucial role in the world's ecosystem. They pollinate 80% of the world's plants, including ninety different food crops. In fact, one out of every three or four bites of food you eat is thanks to bees!

HOW TO BEE A HERO!

Honeybees have lived on Earth for twenty-five million years and are ideally adapted to their natural environment. But due to habitat loss, climate change and the use of some toxic pesticides, their colonies are disappearing around the world.

Here are some ways you can help honeybee populations:

❀ Plant a range of flowers in your garden, or in pots and window boxes. Honeybees especially love wildflowers, such as primroses and marigolds, and other flowers rich in nectar, like lavender.

❀ Become a beekeeper! Not only is beekeeping a fun and exciting hobby, you get to collect and eat your own honey too!

❀ If you see a swarm of bees, don't go near

it, but contact your local authority, who will arrange for a local beekeeper to collect the swarm and take it somewhere safe. Swarming is a natural process when colonies of honeybees increase their numbers.

❀ Buy honey that is produced locally to support the honeybees and beekeepers where you live.

❀ Encourage your local authority to create more bee-friendly spaces, not only in parks and woodland, but on roundabouts, in town centres and roadside verges.

❀ Chat to your family, friends and classmates about how amazing and important honeybees are. The more people know, the more they will do to try to protect them.

Emma Beswetherick is the mother of two young children and wanted to write exciting, inspirational and enabling adventure stories to share with them. Emma works in publishing and lives in south-west London with her family and two ragdoll cats, one of whom was the inspiration for Thunder. *The Honeybee Treasure Hunt* is her sixth book.

Find her at: emmabeswetherick.com

Anna Woodbine is an independent book designer and illustrator based in the hills near Bath. She works on all sorts of book covers from children's to adult, classics to crime, memoirs to meditation. She takes her tea with a dash of milk (Earl Grey, always), loves the wind in her face, comfortable shoes and that lovely damp smell after it's rained.

Find her at: thewoodbineworkshop.co.uk